About the Author

Shaan Ranae brings a sweet taste of romance mixed with some spice, to add some flavor to each of her gritty tales of love. She wishes to take her readers on an emotional journey to find the extraordinary in the ordinary. She's a firm believer, there is something special in all of us.

Tucked Away on Christmas: A Christmas Short

Shaan Ranae

Tucked Away on Christmas: A Christmas Short

Olympia Publishers
London

www.olympiapublishers.com
OLYMPIA PAPERBACK EDITION

A CIP catalogue record for this title is
available from the British Library.

ISBN: 978-1-80439-885-2

This is a work of fiction.
Names, characters, places and incidents originate from the writer's
imagination. Any resemblance to actual persons, living or dead, is
purely coincidental.

First Published in 2024

Olympia Publishers
Tallis House
2 Tallis Street
London
EC4Y 0AB

Printed in Great Britain

Dedication

You. Remember to believe in you... I always will...

Acknowledgements

To my family, the love I have for you will always be my
inspiration.

Every year, it was the same thing. Working overtime to buy useless gifts my family would eventually just return for something else they wanted. People hustling about to purchase the perfect gift that didn't exist.

My daughter could buy herself anything she ever wanted, but I had to continue the tradition. Andy and I promised to always keep the gifts special and that promise was made long before he left us. Whether it was willingly or not, he was gone.

It had been five years, since Andy passed away and every single holiday season, when I heard a knock sound on the door, I imagined it was Andy. His child-like wonder around Christmas made the season magical. He dressed up like Santa and brought gifts for the family. He would *Ho... Ho... Ho...* laugh and jiggle his tummy like a bowl full of jelly. In our earlier years, the jelly was fluff, but in our later years, it was all Andy. Unfortunately, that bowl full of jelly caused the widow-maker of a heart attack which took him from me. The guilt of not forcing him to diet broke me. Not only the guilt, but the loneliness. Left with only my memories to keep me at peace.

My daughter was newly married. So, she would come Christmas Eve and spend the day with me. Then she and Chandler would travel to the in laws for her real Christmas. We typically ate breakfast, exchanged gifts then she would beg me to spend the holiday with her in-laws. Chandler's parents were wonderful humans, but I was not ready and I refused to ruin their festivities.

"Next..." A booming voice announced. I peered up at impatient customers and an open register. I trudged my way through the swarm of shoppers for a quick check out. I flopped the garments on the counter top and huffed out a huge breath, "Happy Holidays. Do you have any coupons?"

Oh for fucks sake, I left my coupons in the car. How could I have forgotten the freaking coupons? That's one of the reasons I came to this store in the first place. I rolled my eyes and cursed under my breath. My filter didn't appear to be working. A little bit of shame washed over me with my lack of Christmas spirit, when the cashier answered, "It's okay, it happens all the time, I can wait until you run out and get them."

I knew it was that time of year of hospitality and kindness, but if I was waiting in that line, I would be pissed if some bitch ran out to her car. I couldn't do that to them.

"No, that's okay. It was just twenty percent off and I can use it for a later purchase." I huffed, obviously irritated with the situation, but I completely understood the predicament. I finally peered up at the cashier.

Damn! Every inch of him was on display. His festive red shirt stretched snugly against his sculpted chest. His pants not leaving much to the imagination. My eyes ogled him gratuitously without shame, at least until I reached his handsome face. The man that I had been appreciating was not who I was expecting. He wasn't some rugged stranger. Don't get me wrong, damn he was pretty, but he was half my age and for goodness sake, I knew him

The recognition had both of us red faced. I felt like a cougar stalking her prey. My hormones must be raging. Who knew with this perimenopausal bullshit? He knew I was checking him out. Sadly, what could I say to get out of this situation? I've known this kid since high school. He spent many years at my house hanging out with my daughter. He harbored a crush on her for years. There were times, he sat and waited for her to come home for hours. I felt bad for the kid. He spent more time with me than her. She was oblivious.

Hannah was gorgeous. Her long blonde hair fell down her back in loose waves. She was a natural beauty. Most people say she was a miniature version of me, but with Andy's crystal blue eyes.

When Andy passed, Tucker was a godsend. He comforted us and helped around the house the first few weeks. I always thought that one day he would wear her down, but he never did. However, they remained good friends to this day. I could only imagine what he thought when she met Chandler. He was resilient though... and beautiful.

"So, Hannah mentioned last time we spoke that she'll be in town late the twenty-third," Tuck said. I nodded at the Adonis with brown skin and a sleeve of tattoos peeking out from beneath his tight shirt. His features are more masculine, far different than the sweet lanky kid who used to mow my lawn while waiting on Hannah to get home. He had grown into his body.

His confidence was apparent and he wore his skin entirely too well. I still can't seem to find words to distract myself from ogling the perfect specimen in front of me, but my imagination got the better of me. Images of being pinned to this countertop by only his body and his hands roaming every inch of my skin, taunting me. Oh hell, I hadn't had sex since Andy passed and my body must've been getting tired of my *battery-operated-boyfriend*. This man caused a reaction within me.

I shook my head momentarily to bring myself back to reality. This kid was my daughter's age. He's young enough to be my son. What the hell was I thinking? Daydreaming about him wasn't bad, but the way I did it was borderline obvious. He was probably used to being objectified by old ladies all the time. My blush made another appearance and I decided to be brave and shove my shame down deep before I responded, "Yeah, she and Chandler will be here on the twenty-third." I nodded awkwardly, embarrassment filled my gut.

"Hopefully, I'll get to see her at the Miller's party on Christmas Eve. She claims she's going," he paused momentarily before gauging my reaction, "Are you planning on going this year?" he asked hopefully. It was endearing. He bit his bottom lip, a tendency of his when he was nervous. The urge to see how good that lip tasted, had me grinding my teeth. His plump lips attracted my eyes. I couldn't stop staring. I caught myself biting my own lip. It felt wrong thinking about him this way. I had known him since he was young, but at the same time my body had its own agenda.

Without trying to commit to anything, I shrugged like it was a possibility. However, I hadn't been to the Miller's party since Andy died. He used to put on his Santa suit to entertain everyone. Sometimes Santa dragged me into a closet for a little fun of our own. Those memories were the hardest during this time of year. I won't be going to the Millers.

"That'll be eighty-six eighteen," he stated sweetly with his Cheshire grin and downturned eyes.

I slid my card into the slot and peered up at the delicious creature in front of me. He was biting his plump lips again. What I wouldn't give for one taste of those juicy… Damn I had to stop this. I forced a polite smile and took my items with me.

I rushed toward the door when he called out my name. I stopped and turned to be met with six feet of hard muscle. Warmth spread through my core. My insides melted from the touch of his chest alone and none of it was purposeful. I wonder what he could do if it were. I dropped my bags and slowly peeled myself off this statuesque man whose lips begged me to nibble on them, but I didn't press the issue. I bravely peered under my lashes to find him staring. Unsure, if I angered or embarrassed him, I apologized sweetly, taking the receipt he waved in his hand. I grabbed my items and charged toward the door so quickly that I probably appeared like a thief attempting a getaway.

Embarrassed and full of shame for my sinful thoughts, I trudged my wobbly legs toward my car, kicking the snow out of my way. How inappropriate was this? I knew his mother. We served in the PTA together and hosted playdates. We helped chaperone the senior prom. Sadly, both of us snuck off and had our own little party with a flask in the teachers' lounge, but at least we were there.

If only I were twenty years younger. He wouldn't know what hit him. Especially now that I was secure in my skills in the bedroom and no longer harbored the shyness that never did me any favors.

I tossed my bags in the backseat, and shut the door. I rested my head on the seat and let go a breath filled with exasperation. Maybe it was time that I started dating again. Maybe it would keep these insane aspirations of affairs with a younger man at bay.

Mentally, I wasn't ready to move on, but physically my body had other ideas. I was so turned on that B.O.B was going to give me a workout later. All while I envisioned his warm brown eyes staring down at me, appreciating my body for what it was. His soft lips pressing against my skin. His hard body giving me the pleasure that I've been aching for.

The heat radiating from my skin fogged my windows and before I had to defrost the entire car, I started the engine.

15

The hues of the red and green streetlights reflected off the wet roads like shimmering highlights. The beauty distracted me slightly from my earlier escapades. Hannah's ringtone filtered through my car speakers and I answered to hear the most precious voice, echoing throughout the car.

"Hey Momma Bear," Hannah announced whimsically. This girl owned my heart. The entire damn thing was hers since Andy left.

"Well, hi babe," I responded in the same chipper tone of voice, "Now, what do I owe for this pleasure." My sarcasm thick, but without ill intention. This became my go to phrase when she called requesting money when in college. She caught onto the irony quickly, giving me a chuckle in response.

A loud huff echoed through the car which alerted me that she had bad news. Did she have something come up? Maybe she decided not to show this year. I wasn't exactly a bundle of joy. When I was about to interrogate her, she confessed, "Mom, would it be a big deal if we came to visit the day after Christmas instead? Chandler's parents rented a cabin from the twenty-third until the twenty-sixth and Chandler really wants to go with them, but we want to make sure that you have somewhere to go. I can't leave you alone on Christmas."

A knot formed in the pit of my stomach at the thought of spending Christmas Eve and Christmas day alone, but at least they weren't trying to make me tag along any more. However, it did hurt a little knowing that they have given up on offering me refuge from my self-induced isolation. At least before, I felt wanted. The back of my throat thickened and tears began to well behind my eyelids. Each passing second threatened sobs, but I choked them back. "Well..."

"Nope! Never mind, it was a stupid question to ask. I'll be there Christmas Eve and meet up with Chandler and his parents later," she announced in a panic. Hannah didn't believe that I was moving forward with my life. She hated the idea of me being alone.

Just because I was a pitiful individual doesn't mean that my daughter needed to be sitting with her sad excuse for a mother on the holiday. I knew she missed her father dearly, especially during this time of year. I would rather she enjoyed the holiday with her new family than sit here with miserable old me. In this case, misery did not love company. I loved her entirely too much to ruin her celebration this year.

"Don't be silly. You know it doesn't matter to me. We can celebrate our Christmas on the twenty-sixth. No problem." I said reassuringly to help ease her mind. Her breath blared through the speakers again. If I know Hannah, she was weighing the words I said and was also wondering if I lied for her benefit. Which I was but who was to say what the truth entailed. However, Hannah trusted me for my word, even if on occasion I fibbed to make her feel better.

"Mom, are you sure?" she pleaded. She sounded like she did when she was a little girl, choosing to go shopping with her friends instead of going with me. It hurt at first, watching my baby girl choose to spend time with others , but wasn't that what we raised them to do? We raised them to leave us. Now I had to let her go.

She would visit but she needed to live her life and her life was with Chandler.

I inhaled deeply to regain my resolve before lying through

17

my teeth, "Of course baby. It's not that big of a deal. Maybe I'll hit the Miller's party on Christmas Eve and get my drink on…" I feigned enthusiasm for the party I've avoided for years, "I'll probably sleep in on Christmas day. It'll be great."

"As long as you're sure. Tell the Miller's that I'm sorry that we can't make it," she quickly changed the subject since she was satisfied with my answer.

My experience from earlier filled my mind. A flash of plump lips filled my mind and warmth engulfed me again. Damn Tucker must've had an overabundance of pheromones or testosterone. "Well, Tucker will be disappointed that you won't be there. I just spoke with him. He's working at Laurel's. He cashed me out."

"Yeah… I heard that. He's the assistant manager. He must have been filling in for the night. From what I hear, Jake, the owner, has taken a liking to Tucker. He has always been such an adult. When the rest of us were getting drunk and dancing on tables, Tuck was the one driving us home and holding our hair back when we puked," she confessed.

I tilted my head back and exhaled a breath, knowing that Hannah had his help on her adventures when she was young brought some comfort. "That boy was always so stupid over you. Honestly one day I thought he'd wear you down." I said trying to help her forget she's leaving me alone on Christmas.

A loud guffaw pierced my ears through my speakers. "Ha… Momma it wasn't me he was stupid over…" she paused laughing like a donkey on the other side of the line, "Tucker crushed severely on you," she blurted Me? That sweet boy who followed my child around like a little puppy had a crush on me? She's insane. What did he see in me? My grouchy behavior when I got off work, when I ran around the house in sweatpants and tank tops? It's not like I was glamourous in any way whatsoever.

"Shut up…" I blurted out in disbelief. I joined my daughter in laughter, however intrigued that sexy… specimen… of a man had a crush on me. Tucker was never the pimply teenager, he had always been handsome, but he was so young. "How do you know that?"

"Mom, didn't you ever notice the way he looked at you? Or maybe the way he would make up reasons to wait for me at the house, while you were home alone. Dad even knew about it. He would tease Tuck about trying to steal his wife. Tucker loved dad, but he had a serious crush on you. He thought you were the ultimate milf."

Oh, my goodness that word annoyed the hell out of me. Totally callous and unattractive, but I still felt slightly complimented by the gesture. Well, hot damn… that embodiment of sexy wanted this old lady. "That's insane! I'm old enough to be his mother." I confessed partly to dismiss the notion and partly to remind myself that he was literally half my age. I might have to repeat the phrase in my head to keep myself from having these impure thoughts any longer.

"Momma, you're beautiful. I wish you could see yourself how we all see you." Her sweet nature melted my insides and I was so thankful for her. Honestly, I hadn't been able to see myself as anything other than Hannah's mother, since Andy's been gone. We had been together for so long, that our identities were intertwined. There was no Hazel without Andy. We were a pair… partners in crime. I didn't even turn my head in another direction since I was so smitten with him. The sadness of missing my best friend, overwhelmed me. Luckily, I pulled into the driveway when Hannah called out my name. "Mom?" she asked.

"Sorry babe, we must have a bad connection…" I lied, embarrassed about my wandering mind, "Well, I'm home now, I have to carry the bags inside, so I'm going to let you go," I said hoping she wouldn't go on any further. My mood had changed considerably thinking of him. I never thought that I would have to live a life without him.

"Oh okay… well, I'll call you tomorrow with the time we are coming. Okay?"

"Sounds good baby, love you." Reassuring her that I was okay and nothing detrimental happened during our conversation.

"Love you." My girl never ceased to amaze me. Those two words coming from her restored my mood from earlier.

She's so much like Andy. Even though, he's no longer around, I get glimpses of him through her. It's a blessing and a curse at the same time. I loved when I heard from my girl, but usually after our talks, I missed him more. The idiosyncrasies that drove me insane in the past were now the things that I missed the most. Even when we argued over menial things like remodeling the house, which failed in comparison to a life without him.

I shook my head to rid myself of the self-induced sadness and exited my car. I opened the back door to reach for the bags in the backseat. The ground slick from the latest freeze caused my feet to slide, I grasped tightly onto my car door to regain my balance. I cursed loudly enough that Mrs. Lemon peered out her bay window decorated with red and green lights. She waved someone down and Mr. Lemon came running out the door, calling my name.

"Hazel dear… are you okay?" the sweetest seventy-five-year old man in the world asked. He rushed to my side and grasped ahold of my arm like a true gentleman before continuing, "Do you have your balance dear?"

Half embarrassed I nodded, "Yes thank you… thank you so much. You shouldn't be holding me up, shouldn't I be the one helping you?" I laughed. He was strong for his age and I allowed him to help me center my gravity. It probably wasn't a good idea to wear my pumps out in the dead of winter.

"Nah, don't think anything of it. It's not often I get to hold a beautiful young woman in my arms," he chuckled like the geriatric Casanova that he was.

I peered over at him in shock and asked innocently, "What about Mrs. Lemon?"

"Oh Agnes is the love of my life, but she's no spring chicken. Long ago, she had legs that went on for days. Now, the only thing that runs for days is her yapper," he jested. They were a cute couple and the best neighbors anyone could have asked for. After Andy passed, he helped me around the house. He did a way better job than Andy ever had. The thought saddened me a little and Mr. Lemon must've seen the change, because he patted my shoulder and said, "listen young lady, he wouldn't want you to be alone all the time, I know when my time comes, I want Agnes to find herself another chump to hear her yapping…" he paused before elbowing my arm, "and if she goes first sweetheart, I'm comin' a courting." He boasted causing a giggle to leave my lips in return.

"Well, I'll keep that in mind…" I said as I took my bags and turned toward the window Agnes was snooping from, "but I don't think she's going to give you up that easily." I winked at the sweet old man and waved good-bye to both him and his wife when I placed my key in the door.

Like every other time I entered my home, I centered myself before opening the door to the room where I found Andy lying lifeless on the ground. The anxiety overwhelmed me and it took my breath away. So many times, I fought the urge to sell the house and move, but it brought guilt too. I couldn't bring myself to leave our home behind. It was our own personal museum, the story of our lives together and the place we raised the most precious little girl. So many memories lived in these halls. The little knick-knacks and trinkets that filled our home weren't just things, they were our history. I couldn't imagine another family filling this house with new memories.

The tears fell before I even realized they were. The sleeves on my jacket were damp from the salty wetness. Instead of peeling it from my body I allowed it to fall freely onto the floor. I kicked one shoe off somewhere and the other one followed but in the opposite direction. There was no reason to be tidy, it was only me here. I left the bags in a pile by the door when I made it to the wine cabinet and found my favorite flavor of red. I popped the cork, and let the bottle breathe.

I found my favorite satellite radio station and listened to rock ballads blare through the speakers. My feet walked in rhythm to the music, in a pseudo dance of sorts. Grabbing the wrapping paper, I set up a wrapping station at the dining room table. I grasped the bags and placed them on top of the table and danced my way into the kitchen to retrieve the sweet redness.

My favorite song blared through the speakers and transported me into old memories. Andy and I used to dance to this every year on my birthday. I twirled around the dining room and held my now half-full glass of wine as if it were my lover. I sang from the top of my lungs and allowed myself the fantasy of someone craving me. Someone who couldn't stop himself from the desire to touch me… to love me as much as the musician loved the woman in the song. The angst, the lust and the unfortunate aspect that he could never have her. His heart out there for everyone to see and he simply didn't give one fuck about it. His love for her surpassed any sense of humiliation or pride that he had dwelling inside of him.

I wished I could live like that. Free from fear of judgements and allowing myself the enjoyment of doing as I pleased. For years, I've wanted to leave this house which haunted me with memories of Andy and settle on a beach somewhere. It had been my dream to end up with the sun on my skin and my toes in the sand. I could move the shop. Hannah already lived in another state. Nothing kept me here but this house and the memories left behind.

I decided that wallowing in my self-pity won't get the gifts wrapped, so I forced myself to unpack the bags. I released each item from its plastic travel case and laid them out on the table. I couldn't wait to see Hannah's face when she opened the necklace I had made from her father's ashes. A tiny silver ladybug sat on top of a set of wings. Andy called her ladybug for as long as I can remember. It was the only thing that came to mind. I wanted it to signify that she would always have her angel sitting close to her heart. It was shipped to Laurel's specialty from New York.

The bags were empty and there wasn't a sign of the necklace. I picked up each bag again and shook the shit out of each one. Nothing, not one fucking thing falls out. Shit! A frustrated growl left my throat. I threw a tantrum fit for a four-year-old, growling and spewing obscenities louder than needed, when I heard a knock on the door.

What the hell? No one came here. Who could that be? Oh shit. I probably scared poor Mr. and Mrs. Lemon. Embarrassment filled my gut and a blush crept up my neck. Humility was a funny thing. I dared not ever upset the Lemon's but truthfully there were not many others, I cared about upsetting at all.

After Andy died, I didn't mind being an asshole for no apparent reason and somehow, I still got away with it. It was a superpower of sorts. My only concern was when the superpower wore off, would I be considered a sad old widow who needed to get a grip.

I tucked my chin to my chest in hopes I might get a little sympathy for my behavior. I inhaled deeply and let every ounce of air enter my lungs before answering.

I opened the door, expecting a little old man with a disappointed look upon his face, but instead I'm met with chocolate brown eyes staring intensely into mine. A shy smile spread across those plump lips and my eyes were once again drawn to the beautiful man in front of me. I stood there for a moment ogling the handsome creature. My hormones ceased all brain activity when it came to him, because I didn't want to feel like an old cougar chasing after young tail. Although it was one fine ass tail at that.

"Well…" I paused trying to regain some composure, "Hi Tucker…" I said politely, trying to act like I was not some sad spinster who found a younger man desirable. I was sure he was used to women making eyes at him but not from his friend's mother.

"Hey…" he responded quietly peering down at the ground

and back up at me, "You left this at the store when you hurried off." He extended his sculpted arm which held a small plastic black bag with Laurel's logo on it, *the necklace.* Relief filled my soul and I was elated.

"Oh Tuck, you're a life saver," I wailed wrapping my arms tightly around his rock-hard waist. I felt every muscle he had carved into his abdomen, pressed against mine. He wrapped his strength around me in return, engulfing me in comfort. It had been years since I've been wrapped in a man's embrace. An attractive man's embrace at that. He smelled like soap and a lightly scented cologne. It didn't take away from the rugged scent of his skin.

I'm holding on tight and his hold mirrors mine. He was such a good guy. Hugging an old lady in her hour of need. Reminding myself that he was too young for me, I released him from my grasp. "Thank you Tucker, you are a hero. This necklace is Hannah's Christmas gift. It's irreplaceable. I couldn't get another one if I tried. Please come in. It's freezing out there." My desperation must've been obvious. He peered down on me with kind eyes and a little something else I wasn't sure of.

"It's not a big deal. It just gives me an excuse to come visit you." The blush that warmed my cheeks had to be obvious to him, I felt like I was on display. He followed me into the dining room. Thank goodness, he was following me because I wasn't so sure that I could keep my eyes from devouring every inch of him. His bashful grin perfectly in place the entire time.

"Would you like a drink? Coffee? Tea? I have a little wine left..." I offered realizing that I probably shouldn't be drinking around him. However, he was a grown man. He could drink wine if he wished. Was it him I'm worried about or is it me? I might say something wrong. I tended to lose my filter when I had been drinking.

"Wine sounds nice. That should warm the old bones up," he jested playfully. What would he know about old bones? I scoffed and waved my hand in his direction motioning for him to have a seat at the table.

"I'll grab the wine and you can make yourself comfortable." I announced heading toward the kitchen to get his glass of wine and to top mine off as well. I had just enough left to fill each glass to my standard of full.

Hopefully he didn't judge my standards versus society's.

With a glass in each hand, I traipsed myself carefully not to spill the red wine all over my cream-colored rug. The urge for delicacy had me tiptoeing across the floor. Sadly, I didn't think this through, since I'm half tipsy and off balance. What made matters worse was that I felt like I'm on display. Like every movement I made was carefully tracked. It was a different dynamic than I'm used to.

I viewed his broad shoulders and chest that stretched out his shirt. Each little crease that pressed against the fabric gave the illusion that with the slightest tug could turn into small tears in the material. His quiet confidence was apparent from his square shoulders and his eyes focused directly on me. He wore his skin well. He was comfortable with who he was. I found myself staring. When my lustful eyes finally discovered his chiseled jaw, which flexed dramatically when he caught me ogling him again. He didn't appear annoyed or embarrassed. In fact, he appeared to be enjoying my pitiful display of awkward ogling.

In an attempt not to seem like a spinster in heat, I acted like he didn't affect me. His brown eyes traveled my body, warming every inch of mine. I pretended that my insides weren't melting. Like every nerve ending wasn't on fire. That his lips weren't causing me to press my thighs together to ease the ache they caused. It wasn't like I could do anything to ease the discomfort. One glass of wine and a lot of self-control was all I needed to make it through the next half hour without making myself look like an idiot.

After a second bottle of wine, Tuck and I sat on the sofa in the living room with rock ballads serenading us through the speakers. We faced one another and laughed at one of many college stories, he had been entertaining me with for the past two hours. He was not the innocent young man I pegged him to be.

However, the level of maturity he possessed for his age surprised me or I misjudged my own. I haven't laughed this much in years. His brand of humor that balances on the edge of dry and goofy is the perfect blend of entertainment.

It was sad, but at this point I didn't even pretend not to fan girl over him. He's perfect, he wasn't perfect by the definition of the term, but he was the authentic charismatic version of himself. I couldn't think of another term to explain when every piece and part of a person just works.

The imperfections that he might view as flaws were the features which separated him from the rest of the world. Those qualities, like his one tooth that stuck out a millimeter more than the rest of his teeth or the freckle that sat just below his left eye that disappeared when his crooked smile made an appearance, weren't blemishes to his features at all, they were enhancements. Small little details that made him… him.

In my inebriated state, I couldn't hold myself back from asking, "So, why aren't you with some beautiful girl right now? I'm sure you have better things to do than sit here with me." I chuckled as I blurted out the question. *Yes, folks the filter has been busted… I repeat the filter is no longer functioning.*

27

He tilted his head toward the ground for a moment, then peered up at me with warm eyes. He rubbed his chin methodically before answering. His smooth baritones commanded my attention, "I'm enjoying myself here," he said simply stating facts. No undertone or innuendo to show playfulness, just honesty on his terms, "How could I not? I'm sitting here, captivated by a beautiful woman. I can

guarantee that I wouldn't want to be anywhere else right now." He placed his hand on my knee and his warmth invited me closer.

I held my breath. It felt foreign yet so enticing. It had been over twenty years since another man had touched me. It had been twenty years since I felt this rush of the unexpected, the excitement of feeling desired by someone. Twenty freaking years... I finally inhaled a breath and noticed they became more rapid as my gaze remained on his face. I felt the heat creep up my neck. His eyes hadn't left mine and he leaned in closer. His warm breath danced across the skin of my lips, "I've wanted you for as long as I can remember." I'm drunk... stupid drunk not only on the wine but on his words. The effects of the wine started burning off the minute, he placed his hand on my leg and had me panting like a dog in heat, but his words were intoxicating.

He was so close that I could almost taste the mixture of wine and mint on his breath. His lips teased mine with proximity, but never quite closed the distance. A strategic move he must've mastered since I'm falling for every single bit of it. It was arousing. It was sexy. It was unreal. I had never been teased so much in my life.

He moved his hand from my knee, to join his other cradling my face in his capable hands. Gentle yet unyielding and firm. His eyes questioning, appearing to be waiting for a sign to move forward. The whole scene had the area between my thighs aching. My heart pounded. My chest heaved to the point that it grazed his with every rise of mine. He was a man of few words, but his intentions were clear.

He was leaving the decision up to me. He would give me what we both wanted right now, but it all depended on me. My control wavered. I had been dreaming about those lips on me for hours and now here was my chance.

What was one little kiss?

I peered up at him with a little trepidation and a lot of hunger. He remained steady teasing me with his lips, millimeters away from mine. His breath dusted my skin, but when his tongue peaked out to wet the softness that I had been wanting on my skin, I was helpless to hold back any longer. If I was going to do this, there could be no regrets. No worries about a future or consequences. It had to be about the moment. The gratification my body had been begging for since seeing him this afternoon. The release I had been needing for quite some time.

I no longer had propriety holding me back, so fuck it. I pressed my lips to his hungrily, like I was trying to devour him. Although, he held me steady, absorbing my attack. A moan left the back of his throat and I could tell he was being cautious, but the sound urged me on. I tugged slightly on his bottom lip with my teeth, leaned back and moaned into his mouth. He let go of my face and grasped my waist. He pulled me on top of him until I straddled his lap and pressed my chest into his. I allowed him to take control of the kiss… of me. I was at his mercy because I wasn't sure what to do with someone new.

His lips caressed mine slowly before he pulled back.

"Look at me…" he whispered while trailing his fingers down the side of my jaw. He searched my eyes. I wasn't sure what he was searching for, but he must have gotten his answer when he pressed his mouth to mine. His movements were sensual and slow. Methodical like he had been planning each motion out in his mind. Like he knew exactly where to tease me next and how to arouse me to the point of combustion.

He trailed kisses down my jaw, nibbling and tasting my skin freely, while he made the most delicious sounds. I was overwhelmed with sensation. I no longer could control my movements. My hips pressed against him searching for something… anything to relieve the ache between my legs.

When I found something firm and unyielding pressed against the ache that needed to be sated, it caused me to gasp in his mouth, which urged him to clutch my hips and control my motions with his hands. He brought me closer and wrapped his arms around me, holding me in place against him. He allowed me to feel every glorious inch of his arousal and every rigid inch of his body. He appeared to be attempting to control himself.

I tilted my head back and a moan emanated from the back of my throat. His lips assaulted my neck like a rabid animal. His teeth grazed and gripped my skin. His hands roamed my body, exploring every hill and valley that landscaped my frame. Sensation overcame me and the desire in his eyes erased any insecurities, I had over my appearance, like the stretch marks from giving birth or the wear and tear the years had left on my body never existed. He didn't appear to notice any marks.

He pulled away from me, placing me on the couch. He stood in front of me with a noticeable tenting of his pants. The curiosity of what he might look like underneath his clothes, had me reaching. However, instead of me grasping ahold of him, he swooped me up in his arms. His eyes stared into mine and with a gruff sounding voice, "Bedroom."

I couldn't even think of anything else when he started

carrying me up the stairs. He did it with ease, like I weighed nothing, but it honestly was true testament of his strength. My eyes searched him for any imperfections and my hands followed them to investigate further. No luck finding one, but I caressed every inch of his thick arms and strong abdomen.

He slid my door open with ease like he had done this a thousand times before. At this point I couldn't care less, I wanted him. His lips were like a drug. They tasted like mint and when they pressed against my skin, the sensation was heavenly. I felt my back hit the bed, which caused a deep inhalation of breath.

He stood above me, staring down at me with his heated gaze. Warmth spread throughout my body and all I wanted was his weight pressed against me. He unfastened the top two buttons off my dress and became impatient, tearing it free. A moan escapes my lips. That was honestly the hottest thing I had ever seen. I felt wanton... sexy.

He released one button at a time from his shirt, teased me with little peeks of his soft brown skin that begged me to touch it. He relaxed his arms letting it fall to the floor. The perfection in front of me was intoxicating.

I couldn't believe this beautiful specimen of a man wanted me. What did he find so desirable? I stopped second guessing my decision when his weight pressed me into the mattress. He's firm and unyielding, yet gentle. His touch alone had my nerves firing endlessly.

We were a mess of limbs and moans. His lips traveled my body like a distinguished explorer marking each territory as his own personal playground. His tender admiration for the body, that I found to be a far less version than it used to be, brought him a sense of pleasure, and the turn on was euphoric. His eyes devoured me. His fingers caressed me. His arms held me. His lips tasted me. I was in sensation overload and it had only begun.

Warmth heated my face, illuminated my skin and caused my eyelids to peek open. A delicious ache radiated between my legs and pulsated throughout my whole body. I definitely had a workout last night. A marathon of Olympic sex. At one point I couldn't tell where I ended and he began.

After the workout he gave me last night, no wonder he's exhausted. Unfortunately, I had never been a person to sleep in. My body had its own internal clock and didn't alleviate from the routine. It could have been a blessing when I forgot to set the alarm, but also a curse when I tried to relive my youth.

I slipped out of bed, tiptoeing to the bathroom to warm my bones in the shower. He's wrapped up in the sheet like a burrito, so I had to sneak into the bathroom completely commando. I caught a glimpse of myself in the mirror and wondered what he saw, I wasn't sure what he would think of me in the light.

Under the soft lighting last night, I was sure some of the sagging and scarring could've been hidden, but now it was all on display. I've aged accordingly for someone who hasn't had a lick of plastic surgery and Botox treatments.

The nozzle of the shower squeaked when I turned it on. I winced. I was not sure why I did that. I doubt the sound could wake a sleeping bear, let alone the sleeping man on my bed. His performance last night could wear out the healthiest of men. I had never been ravaged like that in my life. We threw caution to the wind and allowed our bodies to act out our fantasies. The urge to shut the water off and climb back into bed with that splendid specimen of a man grew. However, my liquid courage wore off somewhere between the second and third time he brought me to orgasm last night.

I forced my feet forward until I felt the tiny beads trickle down my back, leaving goosebumps in their path. It felt so good. The hot water eases my aching muscles. I haven't felt this way in a long time. The delectable ache of satisfaction. The afterglow of feeling wanted. The boost to my ego that I have denied myself since Andy passed.

Guilt rushed over me at the thought of my husband. Having another man in his house... in his bed... touching his wife wasn't something I thought that I would ever do. The tears fell freely until I could no longer decipher the differences between the shower water or my salty regret trailing down my cheeks.

The shower door slid open and a very naked Tuck entered with concern on his face. His arms wrapped around me and held me under the stream of blissful warmth. He rocked and shushed my cries. His grip was gentle yet strong when he grasped my head to peer into my eyes. "What happened?"

Shaking my head, I responded, "Nothing... I just don't know how I feel. Andy was the last man who..." I couldn't finish the sentence. Instead, I leaned into him and sobbed. His quiet reserve impressed me. He showed no remorse, but also didn't take offense to my untimely epiphany. It was so comforting and attractive at the same time. He stood strong for me. I couldn't imagine this display to be a turn on to the man who just spent hours between my legs.

I reached up to wipe my eyes, but his hands beat me to it. His soft lips grazed mine, placed just out of reach in a tease so unbearable that I gave in. Again, I was the aggressor pressing my lips to his hungrily.

He broke the kiss suddenly and trailed them down my face. He opted to hold me instead of allowing me to use him as a way to hide my feelings. After we let the water beat on our skin until it cooled, we left the shower. He dressed me in my robe and wrapped a towel around his sculpted mid-section. In awe of not only his immaculate features, but his kind heart, I stared like a love-sick fool.

If I was only twenty years younger, I could have become enamored with this man. His insanely handsome features mesmerized me. His intellect and kindness baited me further. He was gentle yet commanded the space he occupied. I didn't even think he knew it. He took care of me. I never had anyone take care of me before. I was always the ball busting type – A personality spouse who ran things her way. Andy just came along for the ride. It was a nice to have someone care for me for a change.

I sat on the bed. Tuck knelt in front of me and tucked the hair behind my ears gently. "What are you thinking? Should I go?" he asked so innocently. I peered up into his warm brown eyes and got lost in the memories of last night. I didn't want him to go, but I had to be a realist about what this was. It was one magical night. A Christmas memory that I could live off of for years. Regardless of what happened in the future, I still had this one night. One night that I could keep for me.

"No… let me make you breakfast."

"So, when do you leave for Clearwater?" I asked Tuck after he dropped the bomb on me that he got a promotion and would be managing the Clearwater Location of Laurels. I was partly jealous of his freedom to just go live how he chose and a little saddened that this truly was the last time we would have together.

The syrup had him licking those plump lips and I found it hard to listen to what he said, but I forced myself to attempt to hear the words that left those pretty pillows. "...once I'm settled, maybe you can come visit me?" he paused gauging my reaction. I didn't know what to say. Was he thinking that we had some sort of future? He hadn't even started his life yet and I was the queen of empty nesters.

In an attempt to seem non-committal and not an asshole at the same time, "I'm sure the beach babes will be crawling all over you, but I do love the beach." I chuckled. Trying to keep the mood light and not put too much pressure on any future plans I replied, "Honestly I would love to spend my twilight years walking the beach in the mornings and letting the sound of the waves serenade me to sleep at night. It's been my retirement goal for years..." I paused reminding myself that he just began his career and I planned on retirement. "I'll be the coolest old lady on the beach." I deflected. I was just another story to tell and he told them so well.

"I leave for Clearwater tonight after the party. You could always come stay with me..." he paused to gauge my reaction. I'm stunned. Fear, shame and confusion overwhelmed me. What could he possibly want from me? If this got out, his mother would never forgive me. I doubted that she envisioned her son bedding a woman twice his age. She would want him to find someone to grow old with him instead of one he had to care for. My daughter wouldn't understand. Her mom and one of her friends shacking up.

His hand caressed my cheek, "You think way too much." He laughed under his breath. "I'm not asking you to marry me, Hazel. I just want you to visit; spend time with me."

So we could add mind reader to his list of credentials. However, I couldn't continue to lead him on, "I just don't see how any of this... us can end well."

"Well, maybe it won't end... Don't you think I am qualified to decide who I spend my time with?" He sounded a little angry and his facial features matched his words. I looked at my feet unsure of what to say. I didn't want to hurt him, but he had so much of his life left. I didn't want him wasting it on me when he could find someone his age.

"Why would you waste the time you have on me? Don't get me wrong, last night was the most memorable night I have had in a long time. Actually, I've never had a night like that in my life. However, what kind of person would I be to take your future away from you? Don't you want to find someone your age who can grow old with you... to have your children?"

Now it was his turn to stare at the ground. He leaned against the counter, his head hung low. Just when I thought that I ruined the moment, he lifted his head up and stared into my eyes with resolve, "Then I guess we better make the best of today."

We spent the day in our underwear doing whatever we felt like doing. We watched cheesy Christmas movies. We cuddled in bed and ate sugar cookies. We made out during the between times when he may have pleasured me with his very capable hands and I returned the favor with ease. This had been the best

Christmas Eve, I have had in a long time. I loved his presence. His smile, his stories, and his sense of humor mesmerized me. I couldn't think of anything else, but him today. The rest of the world had disappeared and Tuck became the center of mine even if it was for one day. He even talked me into going to the Miller's Christmas Eve Party tonight, but I wasn't sure how that would work.

It was freezing outside. I should have worn pants. I couldn't believe I let Tuck talk me into wearing my red Christmas dress. I hadn't felt confident enough to wear it, but when Tuck had me try it on and I saw the look on his face. I was sold. He promised me a secret rendezvous if I wore this dress tonight and after that performance last night, how can I deny him?

He left me a couple hours ago to get ready for the party and promised to meet me there with bells on. I hope he wears something else, because I doubt, I'd be able to control myself if the only thing he had on was bells.

I rang the doorbell and Josh answered the door dressed like Santa, howling *HO HO HO* and took the dish of cookies from my hands. I scanned the room for familiar faces and there were so many that I loved. The Lemon's stood near the buffet grazing and arguing over Mr. Lemon's food choices. The Miller's worked the room, trying to make sure that every guest felt welcome. Then guilt washed over me when I saw Melba. She was Tuck's mother. When I saw her, I didn't think I could look her in the eyes. If she only knew that he spent an entire afternoon in my bed. I doubt she would want to be my friend any longer. I turned to walk in the other direction when I ran into a handsome brick wall.

My body betrayed me as I just stood there forcing my hands to my sides, when he said, "I'm glad you came."

The word *came* had my thighs pressed together, again. The memories of him between them had them aching even more. No man had ever had me so sated.

I caught my breath, "I'm here… now what are you going to do with me." A wicked gleam entered his eyes and a devilish grin had me wiggling, but we were surrounded by so many people. We should've stayed in my bed. I'm sure we would've had so much more fun.

Our banter was interrupted by a familiar voice, "Hazel... I'm so glad you decided to join us." Melba's kindness welcomed me and the guilt surfaced again. "Tuck said he saw you at Laurel's last night and that you may come. I'm so glad you did."

I nodded, "I figured it would be about time to reenter the world again."

Tuck chimed in, "We are so glad you did. Now, would you two lovely ladies like some eggnog?" he charmed us. We both nodded and he made his way toward the bar in the dining room. We watched as he charmed the lady behind the bar as well.

"You know he had the biggest crush on you all throughout high school and the way he's staring at you now. I'm not so sure he's outgrown it."

I laughed, realizing that I was the only one oblivious to this massive crush Tuck had on me. "Well, that would be something, huh?" I scoffed like it was entirely implausible.

She's thoughtful for a moment. "Well, I did always want grandchildren," she paused momentarily then laughed before continuing on, "I guess he could do a lot worse. At least you're a successful woman, who has a good heart. He could do a lot worse, plus girl you still got it. How do you do it?"

Shock had me speechless for a moment, but when Tuck turned around, I had to forget everything she said. "Well, they say the divorce diet is good, but I'd say that the widow diet is simply bar none." She laughed with me until Tuck handed us our drinks.

Our night was spent with friends and extended family. Christmas cheer surrounded us. It's the first time I could stand being around others since Andy had passed. Tuck even found a way to pull me into the bathroom for a secret rendezvous of lips, hands, and tongues. I was pretty sure he kept my panties in his pocket.

I dropped him off at the airport later that night and without my panties, but with tons of memories. I couldn't allow him to change his life for me, but he gave me a gift I will always cherish. He gave me back my youth, a new outlook on the rest of the life I had left, and lastly the realization that I was still desirable. I promised to stay in touch and I will keep my promise. It's the least I could do. He gave me so much more.

After some heavy petting and a reluctant goodbye, I watched as he moved forward with his life. The two-hour drive home was sad and lonely. I wanted to have something to remember him by besides the hickeys he left between my thighs.

I opened the door to my own personal museum that I have treated like my jail cell instead of the castle of memories that we made of it. I crawled into my bed that still smelled like Tuck and vowed not to change my sheets until his scent faded away. I stretched my limbs, still aching from our escapades, when my hand met a crisp sheet of paper. I pulled it close enough to my face and read the script on the page.

Hazel,

Please know that I meant every word I said. Please come visit. My address is two-ten Jeffords Street Clearwater. Anytime you want a break from this place. I would be happy to be your escape. I would be happy to be your reality as well but take things in your time. I will always be here. I'll text you when I land.

Yours Tuck

Hannah arrived the next morning. She couldn't let me spend Christmas alone. "I'm so glad that you went to the Miller's party. Maybe this is a step toward your healing. Maybe even one day you'll date someone." My beautiful girl remarked in relief. I exhaled thinking about the events that led up to the party and gave me the nerve to be brave enough to go.

I blurted a confession before we could dwell any further on the subject of healing, "I'm thinking about selling the house, baby girl. It's too many memories and honestly I think it'll be a good thing for me." She looked confused at first, but then a peaceful look masked her face.

"Momma, I truly understand. Sometimes coming home reminds me so much of Daddy that it hurts. Plus it may be nice to have you close by..." She paused reaching into her bag and pulled out a box wrapped with Christmas tree paper.

I opened the gift and saw a yellow onesie with the words, *Mess with me and you mess with my grandma* written across the front. She and Chandler were going to make me a grandma. I wrapped my arms around my baby girl and squeezed her tightly. It's the best gift I could've gotten. "I'm so happy for you."

She hugged me for a moment and smiled. In return, I handed her the small box with the red bow. She opened it and smiled. "Aw a lady bug... I love it."

"Read the description." I instructed and watched as she realized that she will always have a piece of her father with her. A single tear fell down her cheek and I wiped it clear. We didn't talk about him much, but I'm not sure if it's because of me or she found it too painful, but I had to change that. She smiled and thanked me. We cuddled on the couch and watched old home movies and as we laughed at our memories with Andy, I felt blessed. Blessed that I had a lifetime of love and an unknown future that I had no doubt would bring many more memories to cherish.

"So Hannah, for New Years, I'm thinking of hitting up the beach, so don't worry about me. I'm due for a nice long vacation."

She smiled, "So, which beach are you thinking about heading to?" "Not sure yet, but I hear Clearwater is beautiful this time of year."

The End